The Magic Clock

by Diane Jackman

Illustrated by Tina Hancocks

GONDOLA

In Mrs Harper's toyshop
in the corner of the square
the toys sat and dreamed.
Clara, the ragdoll looked across
the shop at Marietta.
Marietta lived in the musical box,
and when the lid was opened
she danced round and round
on pointed toes.

Clara was a very floppy rag doll
She had floppy arms
and floppy legs.
She could not dance.
Every morning she would try
to lift her floppy arms
and stand on her floppy legs.
But she could not move.
"Oh," she sighed, "I wish
I could dance like Marietta.
But my legs are too floppy."

The toy soldiers stood straight
in their smart red uniforms.
They had trumpets and drums,
but they could not play them.
"Oh," sighed Tom, the smallest soldier,
"I wish we could march up and down,
just like the real band in the square.
But we are too stiff to move."

Edward the teddy bear sat on
his shelf and dreamed.
He always had such good ideas
but could not tell them to anyone
because he could not speak.
"Oh," he sighed, "I wish I could
speak. I could tell everyone about
my good ideas. But the only
noise I can make is a growl,
if someone presses my back."

One morning a package arrived.
Inside was a cuckoo clock.
"It's just right for my shop,"
said Mrs Harper.
She put the clock on the shelf.
"Tick, tock," went the clock,
but as each hour struck,
the cuckoo did not appear.
"How strange," said Mrs Harper.

Clara looked at the new clock
on the shelf.
"A dancing princess must live
in there," she said to herself.
"A fine band must march past,"
said Tom to himself.
"I think I know how to let
the cuckoo out," said Edward
to himself. "But I can't
tell anyone."
Nobody knew the real secret
of the cuckoo clock.

That evening, after Mrs Harper
had closed the shop, the toys sat
and dreamed.
The new cuckoo clock struck
seven o'clock, eight o'clock,
nine, ten, eleven.
The clock struck midnight.
Then the clock began to glow.

The toys looked at the clock
in surprise as the light
filled the room.
The cuckoo came through the door
and called three times.
"Cuckoo! Cuckoo! Cuckoo!"
Clara turned to look at
the other toys and found that
she could move her head.

Then Clara lifted her floppy arms
She stood up on her floppy legs.
She began to dance!
She danced all around the toyshop!
"Look! Look at me!" she cried,
as she danced past Marietta's
musical box. "I can dance,
just like you!"

The lid of Marietta's musical box opened and Marietta twirled round on the tips of her toes. "Not quite like me," she said, as Clara danced past.
Clara did not mind. She just danced and danced.

The toy band marched up and down.
Tom followed, banging away
at his big bass drum.
Edward found he could speak.
"I have a good idea," he said.
"Let's have a party!"
The toys cheered!

The toys used food from the cupboards in the doll's house. They used the doll's tea set. Even Rory, the lazy lion, woke up and ate a sausage. "Do you think this magic will happen again, Edward?" asked Clara. "I want to dance again and again." "I have a good idea that it might," said Edward.

Suddenly, the door on the clock opened.
The cuckoo came out as the first light
of dawn shone through the window.
"Cuckoo! Cuckoo! Cuckoo!"
The toys could not move.
The band stopped playing.
Edward could not speak.
Clara could not dance.
"I wish, I wish . . ." she said to
herself as she flopped against
the doll's house.

Say these words again

floppy	clock
toy	drum
musical box	lazy
trumpet	tea set
growl	toes
magic	secret
dance	princess